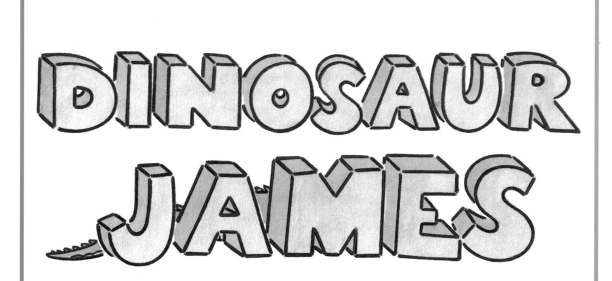

DINOSAUR JAMES

STORY AND PICTURES BY
SCOTT TAYLOR

MORROW JUNIOR BOOKS/NEW YORK

Printed in Singapore by Tien Wah Press.

1 2 3 4 5 6 7 8 9 10

Library of Congress Cataloging-in-Publication Data
Taylor, Scott.
Dinosaur James : story and pictures / by Scott Taylor.
p.   cm.
Summary: People doubt the value of James's dinosaur obsession,
until it helps him deal with the playground bully.
ISBN 0-688-08576-8. ISBN 0-688-08577-6 (lib. bdg.)
[1. Dinosaurs—Fiction.   2. Bullies—Fiction.
3. Stories in rhyme.]   I. Title.
PZ8.3.T218Di   1990
[E]—dc20   89-27268   CIP   AC

To my family

This is our mother

and this is our dad.

This is our dog.   His name is Vlad.

This was our nanny

and this is James.

And he will play nothing but dinosaur games.

James has a room full of dinosaur things:

dinosaur gliders
with dinosaur wings,

dinosaur teddy bears,

dinosaur socks.

Why, he even tells time on his dinosaur clocks.

James has a shelf
full of dinosaur books
with pictures of just
how each dinosaur looks.

He can spell all
of the dinosaur names
and he will play nothing
but dinosaur games.

All of the rest of us wondered why James
would never play any but dinosaur games.
We thought he was odd,
and we thought he was weird,

and we wondered if he could be all he appeared.

"Will you come out to the playground to play?"

"No," says James, "I'd rather stay."

"No," says James, "I'd rather not."

It was always the same.
It was not just a whim.
It was dinosaurs,
dinosaurs ever with him!

He would never come near us,
however we tried.

Could it be that my brother
had something to hide?

who seized him
and teased him
and called him such names!

And all of us felt very sorry for James.

But James did not cry. He did not seem to care.
And James had a very mysterious air.
He said not a word, and he seemed so resigned,

all of us wondered what James had in mind.

And that night, when Muggins
was down at the park,
we heard such a scream
in the gathering dark!

A growl and a gobble,
a gulp and a roar,

and Muggins Malone
does not tease anymore.

So now we leave James to his pleasures reptilian
and no one will tease him—

no, not for a million!

If anyone asks us, we just say, "That's James:

the boy who plays nothing
but dinosaur games."